Moshi Monsters

FANGTASTIC ACTIVITY BOOK

How many times can you spot Hansel hiding in this book?

MY MONSTER

Introducing . . . your very own monster! Use this page to record all the details about your cute, furry or crazy monster. Are you a Moshi member? Add the Moshi passport sticker to your profile!

My Owner Name:

Fave Moshling:

I'm Feeling:

Fave Colour:

Fave Music:

Fave Food:

My Monstar:

MOSHLING GARDEN

This little Luvli is desperate for a pet Moshling of her own. Follow the wiggly lines to work out which one she will catch if she plants these seeds. Stick the Cluekoo sticker next to your answer.

DRAGON FRUIT
BLUE

STAR BLOSSOM
PINK

CRAZY DAISY
PURPLE

4

MONSTROUS MAKEOVER

Dewy's got all you need to give your room a fangtastic makeover in his DIY shop. But you've only got **200 Rox**. Add up the costs of these items and see which pair is within your beastly budget!

A
94   162

B
107   60

C
114   89

ANSWER:

5

PUZZLE PALACE

Attention monsters! Grab a Rock Clock and give yourself one minute to see how many of these puzzles you can solve.
On your paws ... get set ... GO!

SECRET WORD

Which word is hidden in the grid?

A	L	Z	O	P	Q
R	T	L	S	E	A
D	H	G	J	U	Y
V	P	M	A	V	N

Answer:

SCARE SQUARES

How many squares are there?

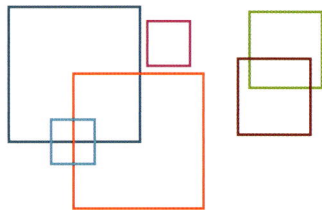

Answer:

THE RED SQUARE

Which symbol should go in the box?

$$2 \;\boxed{}\; 5 = 4 + 6$$

Answer:

NUMBER JUMBLE

Which digit is not present?

7	9	5
3	0	6
2	8	1

Answer:

SUPER SCRAMBLE

Which word can you make by rearranging these letters?

E o s S T r T M N

Answer:

SPELLING SPREE

Which is the correct spelling of this word?

A. BANARNA

C. BANNANA

B. BINANA

D. BANANA

Answer:

CRAZY QUILTS

Which quilt is not a rotated version of the others?

A.  **B.**

C.  **D.**

Answer:

CHOCK·A·BLOCK

How many cubes are in this shape?

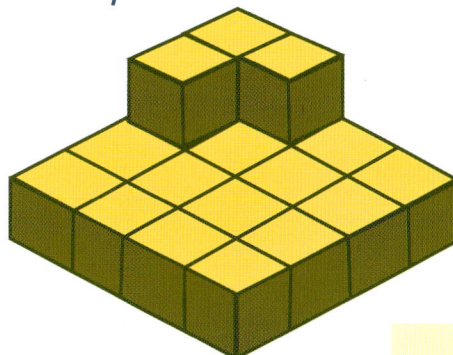

Answer:

7

MESSAGE IN A BOTTLE

Cap'n Buck E Barnacle is at sea with this coded message. Use a mirror to help him decode it, then use the clues to find the treasure. Use a sticky X to mark the answer.

Move two squares north then turn to face the pair of palms. Continue east three squares. The treasure is buried in the square to your south-west.

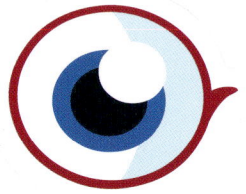

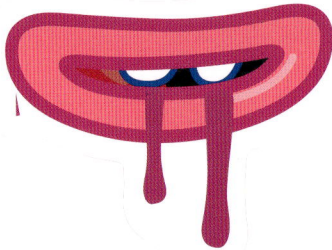

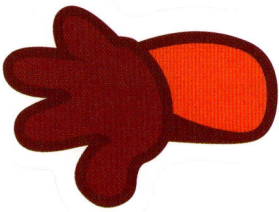
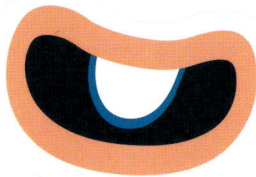
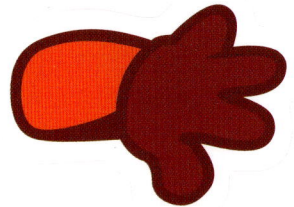

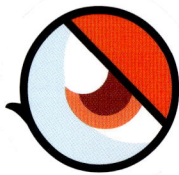

moshi monsters™

SCARY SILHOUETTES

Think you know your monsters? What about your Moshlings?
How many of these can you identify from their silhouettes?

A.

B.

C.

E.

D.

F.

H.

G.

J.

I.

BUSTER'S WORD SEARCH

Buster Bumblechops, Moshling Collector extraordinaire, has misplaced six Moshlings and six Moshi Monsters in this grid! Help him find them all, by searching horizontally, vertically, diagonally and even backwards!

```
A X E L Q E F T G Y J U Y T L
D F R G M I N I B E N V G F U
B G H J Y U J V F D S A Z X V
F D O O N H Y K R F F U T G L
B I G G Y F X A N E I U L H I
A A L L G T R T G I N A R E D
C V D V B N M S P O I U Y I R
F L S A E S Q U I D G E C V B
J O H G T Y F M C V B N C L K
E B G T Y J K A L K J H G T O
E V F Y T U H D E E B G T Y O
P M X P B V C R E I Q W A E X
E O L Z O M M E R D M N B V G
R T J H Y G B V F D T R F D S
S V C D K R O P P O P P E T A
```

PSST! There's a secret extra Moshling hidden in the grid. If you know this sparkly little gem, see if you can find her name!

POPPET	DIAVLO	KATSUMA
JEEPERS	IGGY	ODDIE
ZOMMER	FURI	LUVLI
ECTO	SQUIDGE	MINI BEN

10

MOSHLING MAZE

There are more Moshlings to be found in this maze!
Help this Poppet find her way through from start
to finish, collecting the Moshlings as you go.
Find a zoo sticker for her to keep her Moshlings in!

START

FINISH

MONSTER MASH

Not all monsters are cute and fluffy, you know. Zommer is definitely a little freaky looking. But if you could create your own monster, what would it look like? Use the stickers and your favourite colours to make your own monster here!

FLAG FRENZY

Outside Monstro City there's a big wide world out there! Can you help this Diavlo match the flags to the countries they belong to?

A.

B.

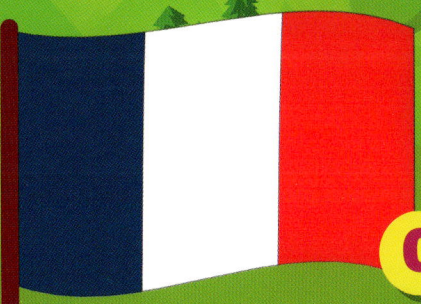

C.

D.

E.

F.

AUSTRALIA

CHINA

SCOTLAND

MEXICO

SOUTH AFRICA

FRANCE

KATSUMA COUNT

There are loads of Katsumas down at the Port. How many can you find?

SUPER SEEDS

ANSWER:

14

THE DAILY GROWL

Roary Scrawl here with BIG news! I'm looking for a new roving reporter to join my team here at *The Daily Growl*, Monstro City's awesome newspaper. So what are you waiting for? Get out there and find me a headline story for this exciting edition – the wilder and wackier the better!

The Daily Growl

ANSWERS

Hansel appears 5 times in this book.

PAGE 4
Moshling Garden
Luvli will catch Cutie Pie.

PAGE 5
Monstrous Makeover
You can afford B.

PAGE 6
Puzzle Palace
Scare Squares - there are 11 squares

Secret Word

A	L	Z	O	P	Q
R	T	L	S	E	A
D	H	G	J	U	Y
V	P	M	A	V	N

The Red Square - **x** goes in the box
Number Jumble - 4 is missing
Super Scramble - MONSTERS
Spelling Spree - D is correct
Crazy Quilts - D is different
Chock-a-Block - 19 cubes

PAGE 8
Message in a Bottle
The message is: Move two squares north then turn to face the pair of palms. Continue east three squares. The treasure is buried in the square to your south-west.

PAGE 9
Scary Silhouettes

A. Katsuma
B. Burnie
C. Poppet
D. Diavlo
E. Tiki
F. Luvli
G. Furi
H. Oddie
I. Jeepers
J. Zommer

PAGE 10
Buster's Word Search
The secret Moshling is Roxy

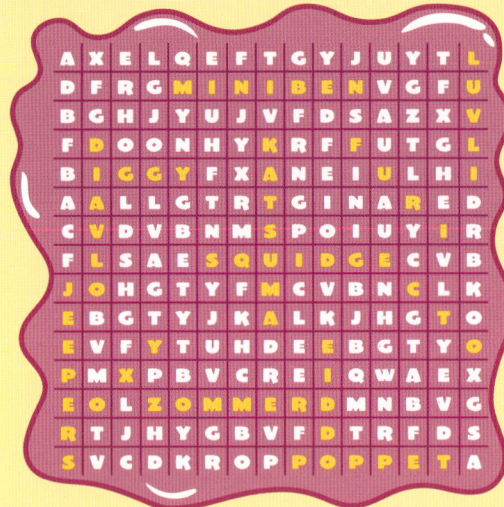

PAGE 11
Moshling Maze

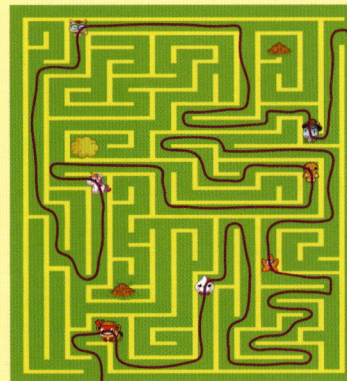

PAGE 13
Flag Frenzy
A. South Africa
B. China
C. France
D. Mexico
E. Australia
F. Scotland

PAGE 14
Katsuma Count
There are 8 Katsumas